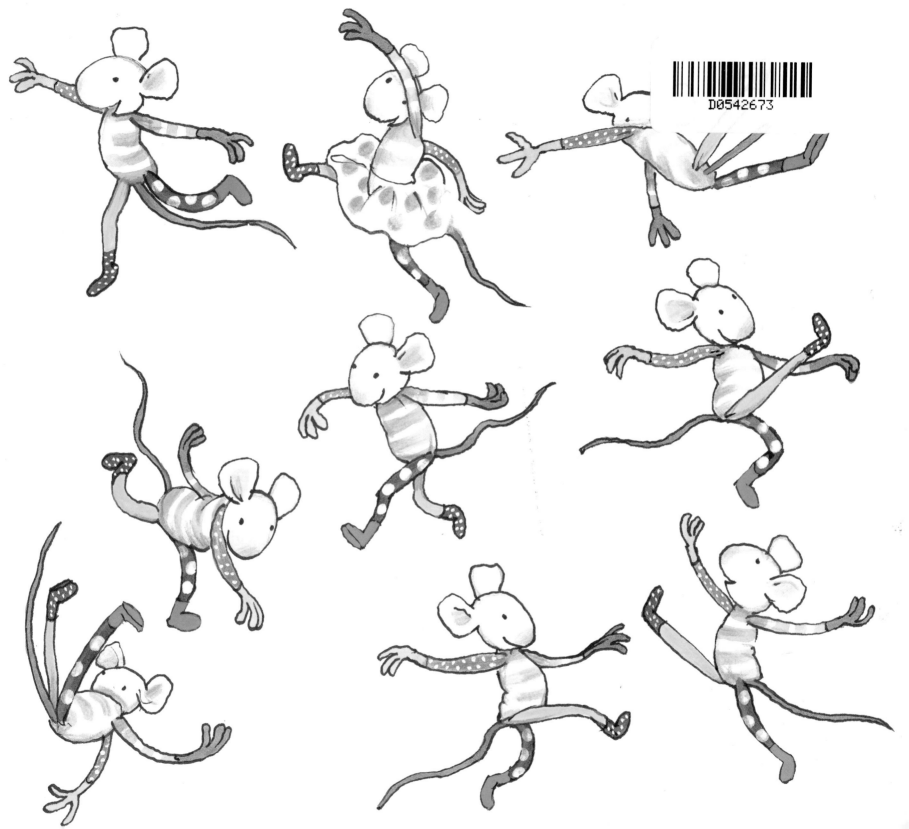

For Ania

TRANSWORLD PUBLISHERS
61-63 Uxbridge Rd, London W5 5SA
A division of The Random House Group Ltd

RANDOM HOUSE AUSTRALIA (PTY) LTD
20 Alfred Street, Milsons Point, Sydney,
New South Wales 2061, Australia

RANDOM HOUSE NEW ZEALAND LTD
18 Poland Road, Glenfield, Auckland 10, New Zealand

RANDOM HOUSE (PTY) LTD
Endulini, 5A Jubilee Road, Parktown 2193, South Africa

First published in the USA in 2001 by HarperCollins Publishers
Published in the UK in 2001 by Doubleday
a division of Transworld Publishers

1 3 5 7 9 10 8 6 4 2

Copyright © Jan Ormerod 2001

The right of Jan Ormerod to be identified as the Author
of this work has been asserted in accordance with
the Copyright, Designs and Patents Act 1988

A catalogue record for this book is available
from the British Library

ISBN 0 385 60236 7

Printed in Singapore by Tien Wah Press (Pte.) Ltd.

# Miss Mouse's Day

*That's me!*

by Jan Ormerod

Doubleday

starts with a cuddle,

then a story.

Then I get dressed.

Too hot!

Too big!

Too frilly!

Just right.

For breakfast I like

strawberries

and eggs

and orange juice

and jam.

Time to wash up.

Then I like to draw.

I use pencils

and crayons,

watercolours

and finger paints.

I can't see. . . .

WOW! It's me!

Dressing up is fun.

Too fancy.

Too spooky.

Too scary.

I like lipstick best . . .

and stars, and stripy socks.

I'm gorgeous!

A little lunch.

Then a little exercise.

Whee!    Oops.    HELP!

Saved!

I'm a very fine slider . . .

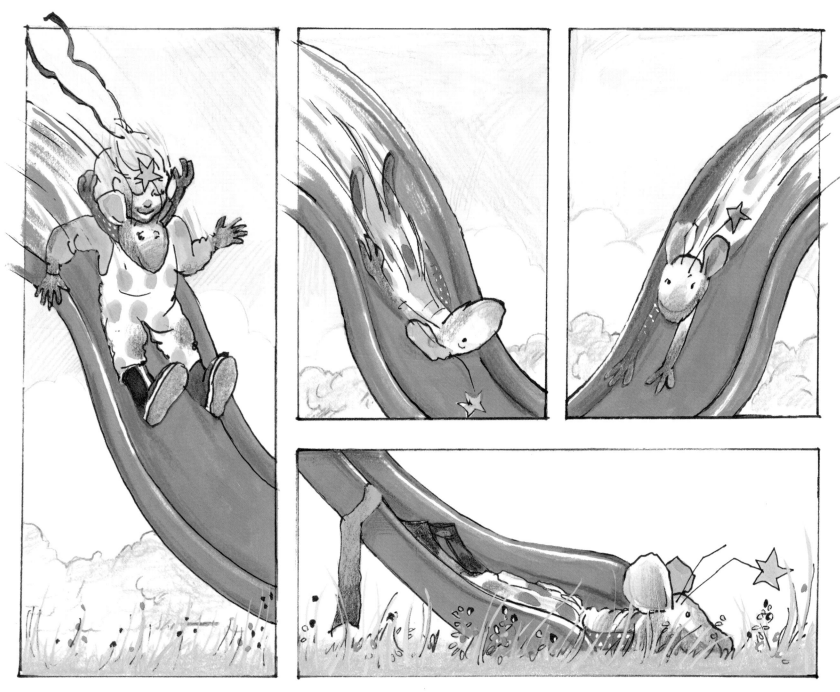

mostly.

I'm a super builder.

Push,

pull,

dig.

A house!

Two houses.      Three houses.

A whole city!

I love flowers

and mud.

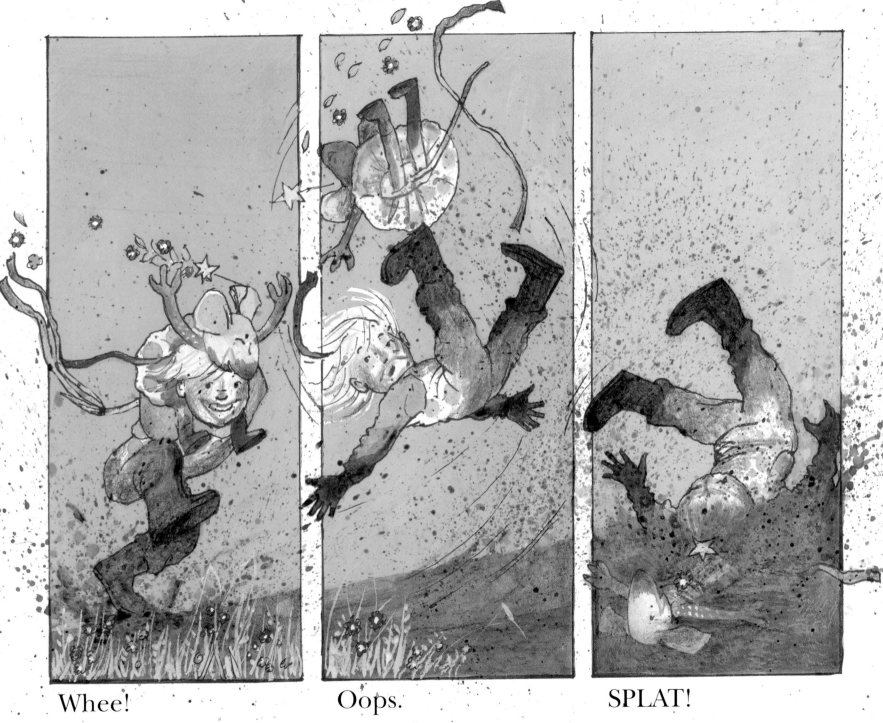

Whee!          Oops.          SPLAT!

"What a mess!

To the tub!"

Oh, dear.                        Don't forget me!                  Uh-oh . . .

**Is that a light?**

**Whew!**

Wash, wring,

towel, spin: clean and dry.

Quiet games

and a story.      A yawn,      then off to bed.

A good night kiss, and my day ends . . .

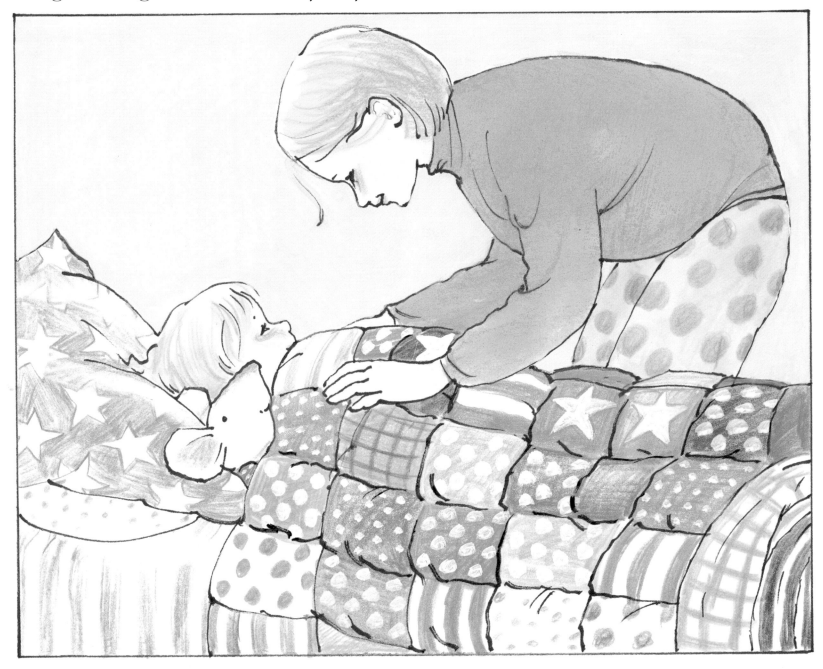

with a cuddle.

*Good night!*